W9-BUC-601

[redacted]

[redacted]

SFORMERS: MOVIE ADAPTATION ISSUE NUMBER ONE

STORY BY ROBERTO ORCI & ALEX KURTZMAN AND JOHN ROGERS
SCREENPLAY BY ROBERTO ORCI & ALEX KURTZMAN

ADAPTATION BY KRIS OPRISKO
ART BY ALEX MILNE
COLORS BY JOSH PEREZ
COLOR ASSIST BY LISA MOORE
EDITS BY CHRIS RYALL

potlight
IDW

Paramount
DREAMWORKS
PICTURES

Licensed by:

Hasbro

Special thanks to Hasbro's Aaron Archer, Elizabeth Griffin, Sheri Lucci, Richard Zambarano, Jared Jones, Michael Provost, Michael Richie, and Michael Verrecchia for their invaluable assistance.

VISIT US AT
www.abdopublishing.com

Reinforced library bound edition published in 2008 by Spotlight, a division of the ABDO Publishing Group, 8000 West 78th Street, Edina, Minnesota 55439. Published by agreement with IDW Publishing. www.idwpublishing.com

TRANSFORMERS, and all related character names and the distinctive likenesses thereof are trademarks of Hasbro, Inc., and is/are used with permission. Copyright © 2008 Hasbro, Inc. www.hasbro.com

All rights reserved. No portion of this book can be reproduced by any means without permission from IDW Publishing, except for review purposes.

Library of Congress Cataloging-in-Publication Data

Oprisko, Kris.
  Transformers : official movie adaptation / story by Roberto Orci & Alex Kurtzman and John Rogers ; screenplay by Roberto Orci & Alex Kurtzman ; adaptation by Kris Oprisko ; art by Alex Milne ; colors by Josh Perez ; color assist by Lisa Moore ; edits by Chris Ryall. -- Reinforced library bound ed.
      p. cm.
  ISBN 978-1-59961-481-6 (v. 1) -- ISBN 978-1-59961-482-3 (v. 2) -- ISBN 978-1-59961-483-0 (v. 3) -- ISBN 978-1-59961-484-7 (v. 4)
  1. Graphic novels. I. Milne, Alex. II. Ryall, Chris. III. Transformers (Motion picture : 2007) IV. Title.

PN6727.O67T73 2008
741.5'973--dc22

                                                                2007033989

All Spotlight books have reinforced library bindings and
are manufactured in the United States of America.

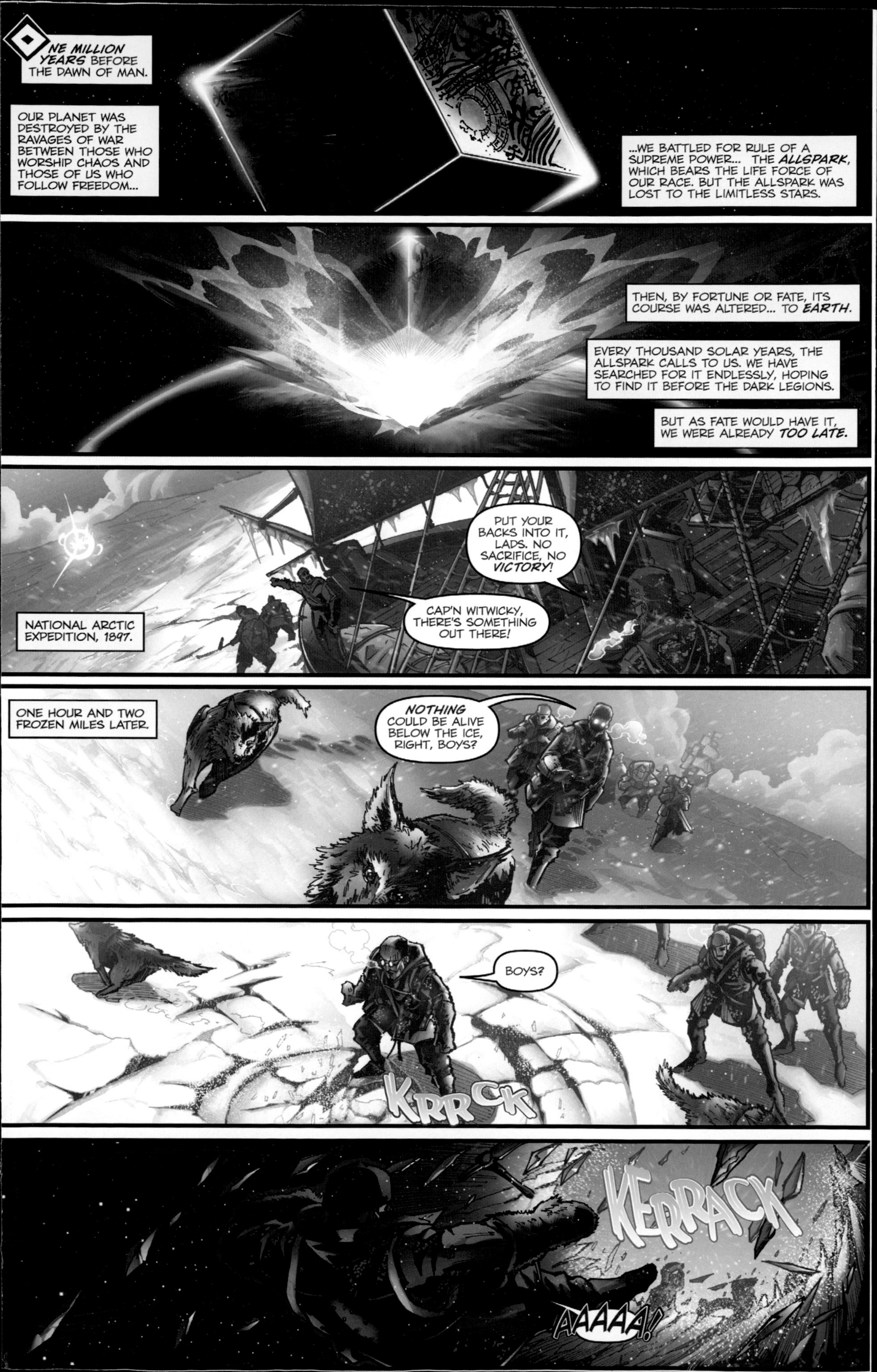
ONE MILLION YEARS BEFORE THE DAWN OF MAN.
OUR PLANET WAS DESTROYED BY THE RAVAGES OF WAR BETWEEN THOSE WHO WORSHIP CHAOS AND THOSE OF US WHO FOLLOW FREEDOM...
...WE BATTLED FOR RULE OF A SUPREME POWER... THE ALLSPARK, WHICH BEARS THE LIFE FORCE OF OUR RACE. BUT THE ALLSPARK WAS LOST TO THE LIMITLESS STARS.
THEN, BY FORTUNE OR FATE, ITS COURSE WAS ALTERED... TO EARTH.
EVERY THOUSAND SOLAR YEARS, THE ALLSPARK CALLS TO US. WE HAVE SEARCHED FOR IT ENDLESSLY, HOPING TO FIND IT BEFORE THE DARK LEGIONS.
BUT AS FATE WOULD HAVE IT, WE WERE ALREADY TOO LATE.
PUT YOUR BACKS INTO IT, LADS. NO SACRIFICE, NO VICTORY!
NATIONAL ARCTIC EXPEDITION, 1897.
CAP'N WITWICKY, THERE'S SOMETHING OUT THERE!
ONE HOUR AND TWO FROZEN MILES LATER.
NOTHING COULD BE ALIVE BELOW THE ICE, RIGHT, BOYS?
BOYS?
KRRCK
KERRACK
AAAAA!

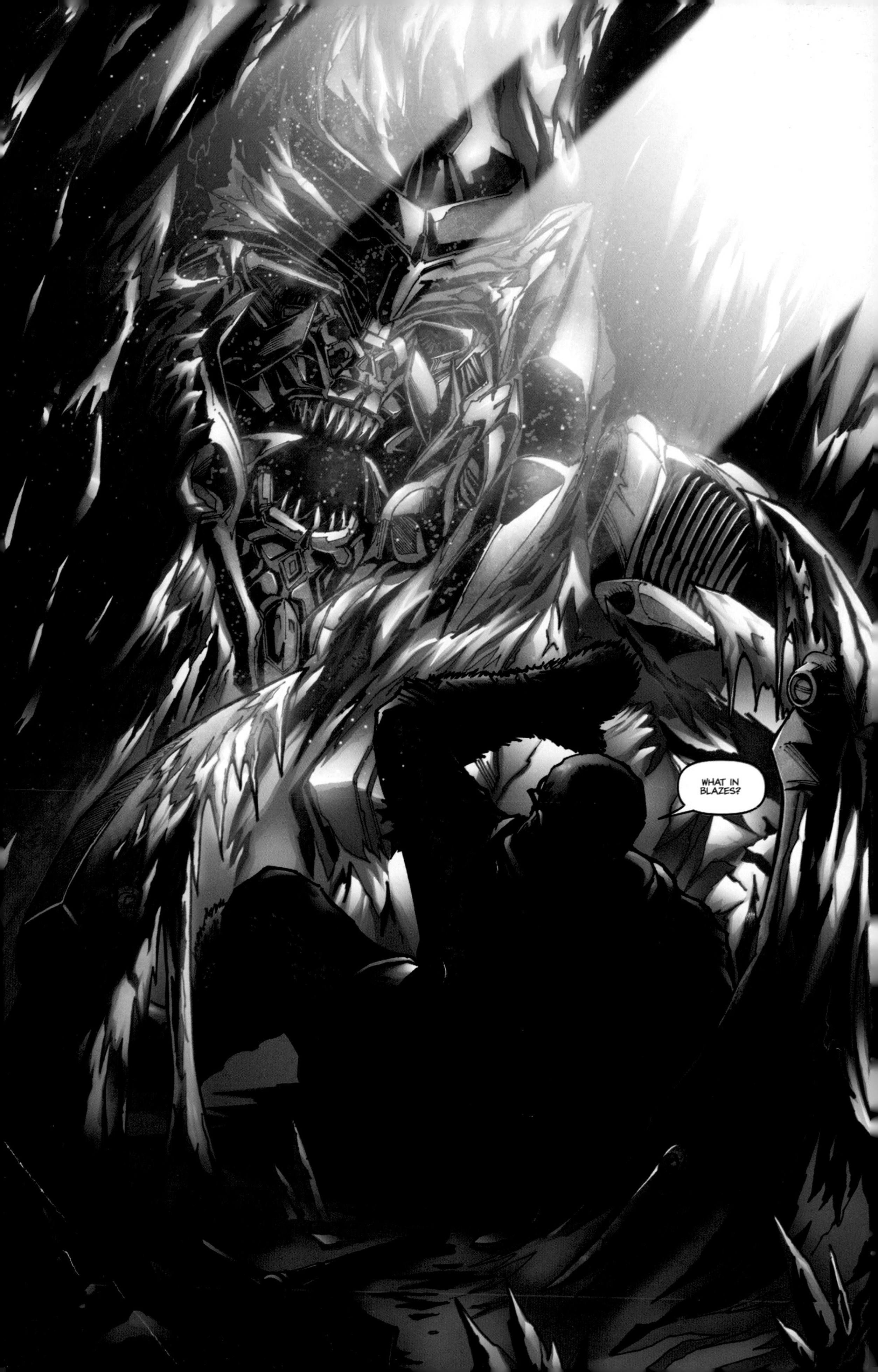
WHAT IN BLAZES?

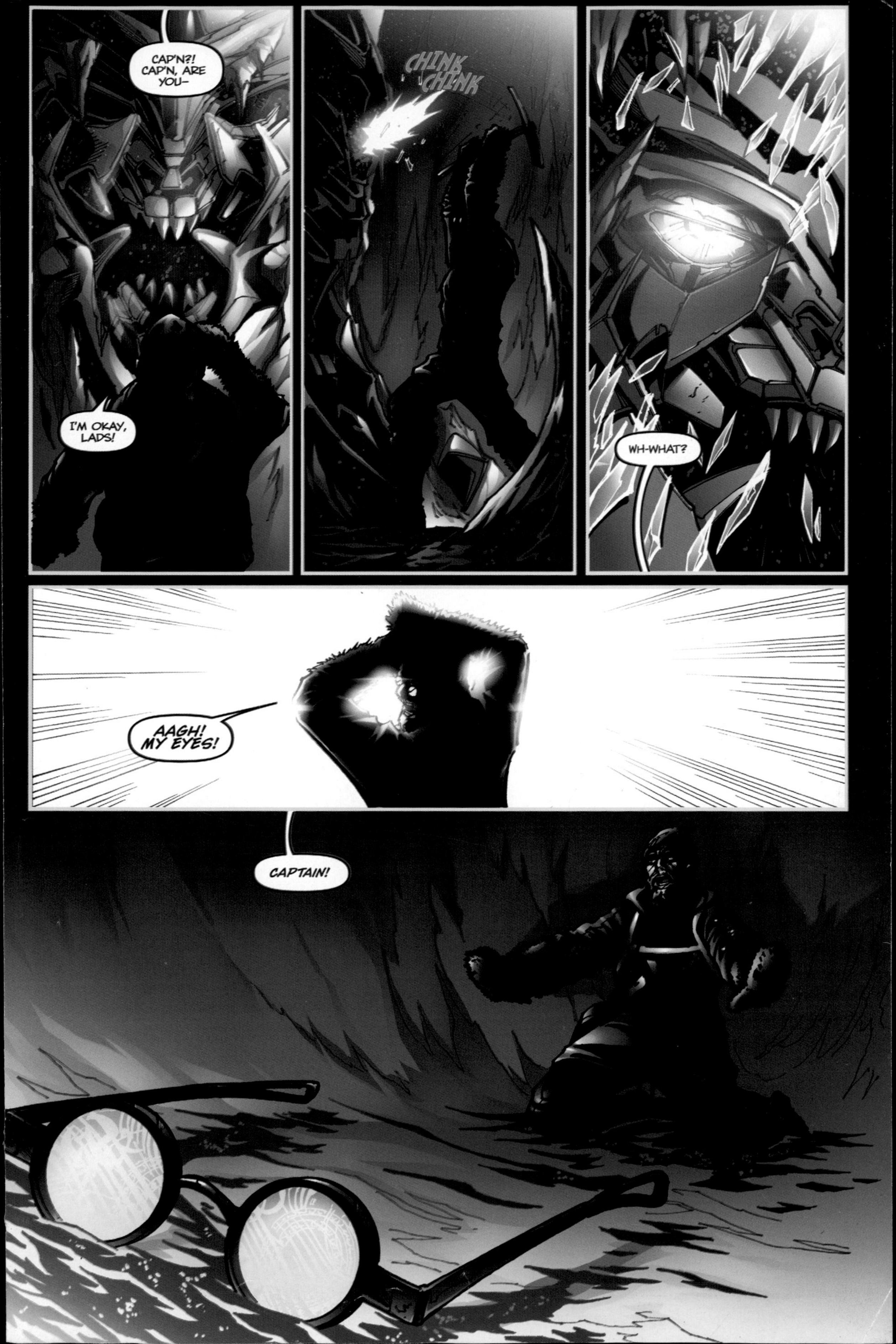
CAP'N?! CAP'N, ARE YOU–
I'M OKAY, LADS!
CHINK CHINK
WH-WHAT?
AAGH! MY EYES!
CAPTAIN!

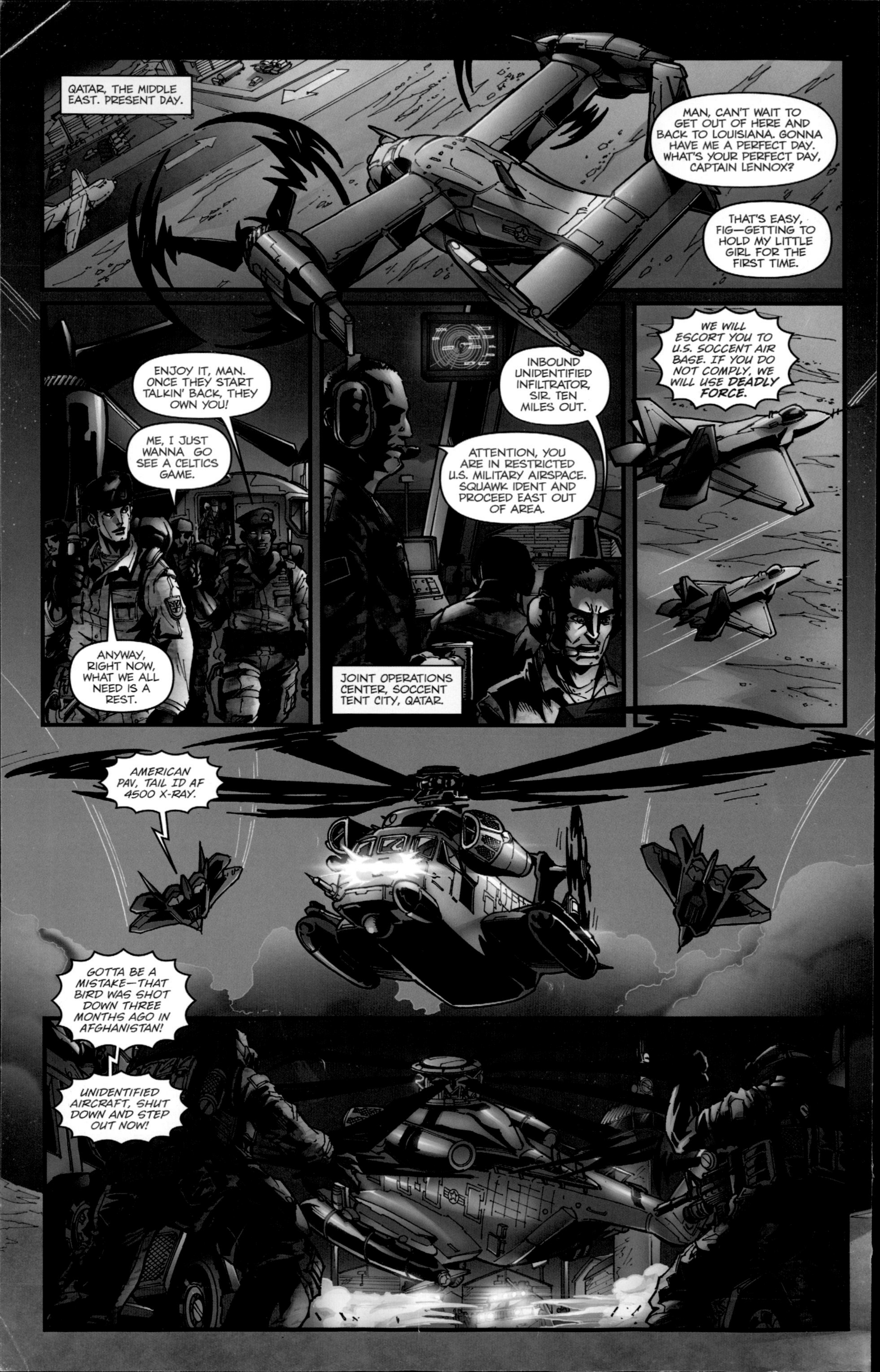
QATAR, THE MIDDLE EAST. PRESENT DAY.
MAN, CAN'T WAIT TO GET OUT OF HERE AND BACK TO LOUISIANA. GONNA HAVE ME A PERFECT DAY. WHAT'S YOUR PERFECT DAY, CAPTAIN LENNOX?
THAT'S EASY, FIG—GETTING TO HOLD MY LITTLE GIRL FOR THE FIRST TIME.
ENJOY IT, MAN. ONCE THEY START TALKIN' BACK, THEY OWN YOU!
ME, I JUST WANNA GO SEE A CELTICS GAME.
ANYWAY, RIGHT NOW, WHAT WE ALL NEED IS A REST.
INBOUND UNIDENTIFIED INFILTRATOR, SIR. TEN MILES OUT.
ATTENTION, YOU ARE IN RESTRICTED U.S. MILITARY AIRSPACE. SQUAWK IDENT AND PROCEED EAST OUT OF AREA.
JOINT OPERATIONS CENTER, SOCCENT TENT CITY, QATAR.
WE WILL ESCORT YOU TO U.S. SOCCENT AIR BASE. IF YOU DO NOT COMPLY, WE WILL USE DEADLY FORCE.
AMERICAN PAV, TAIL ID AF 4500 X-RAY.
GOTTA BE A MISTAKE—THAT BIRD WAS SHOT DOWN THREE MONTHS AGO IN AFGHANISTAN!
UNIDENTIFIED AIRCRAFT, SHUT DOWN AND STEP OUT NOW!

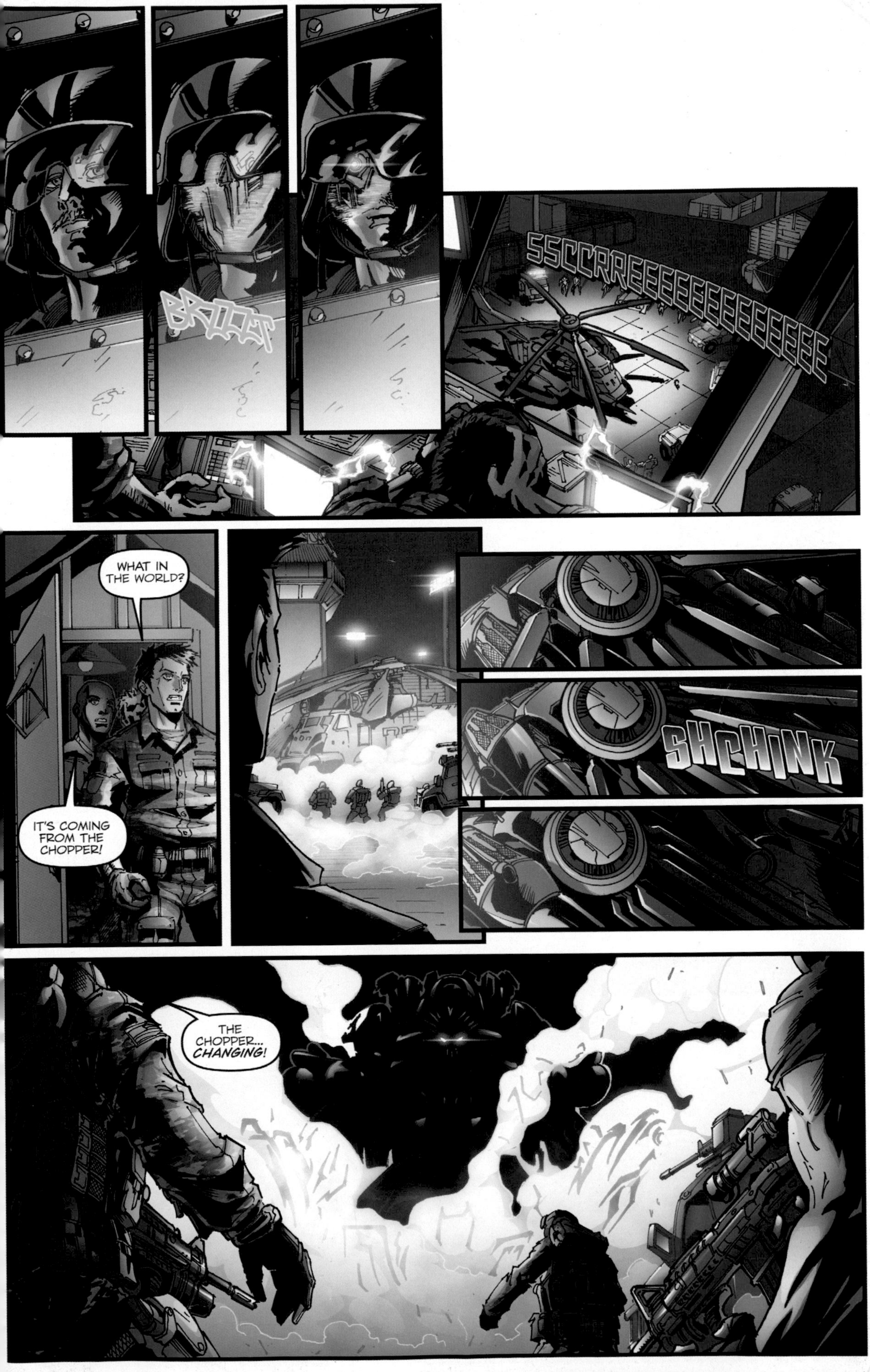
BRZZZT
SSCCRREEEEEEEEEEEEEE
WHAT IN THE WORLD?
IT'S COMING FROM THE CHOPPER!
SHCHINK
THE CHOPPER... CHANGING!

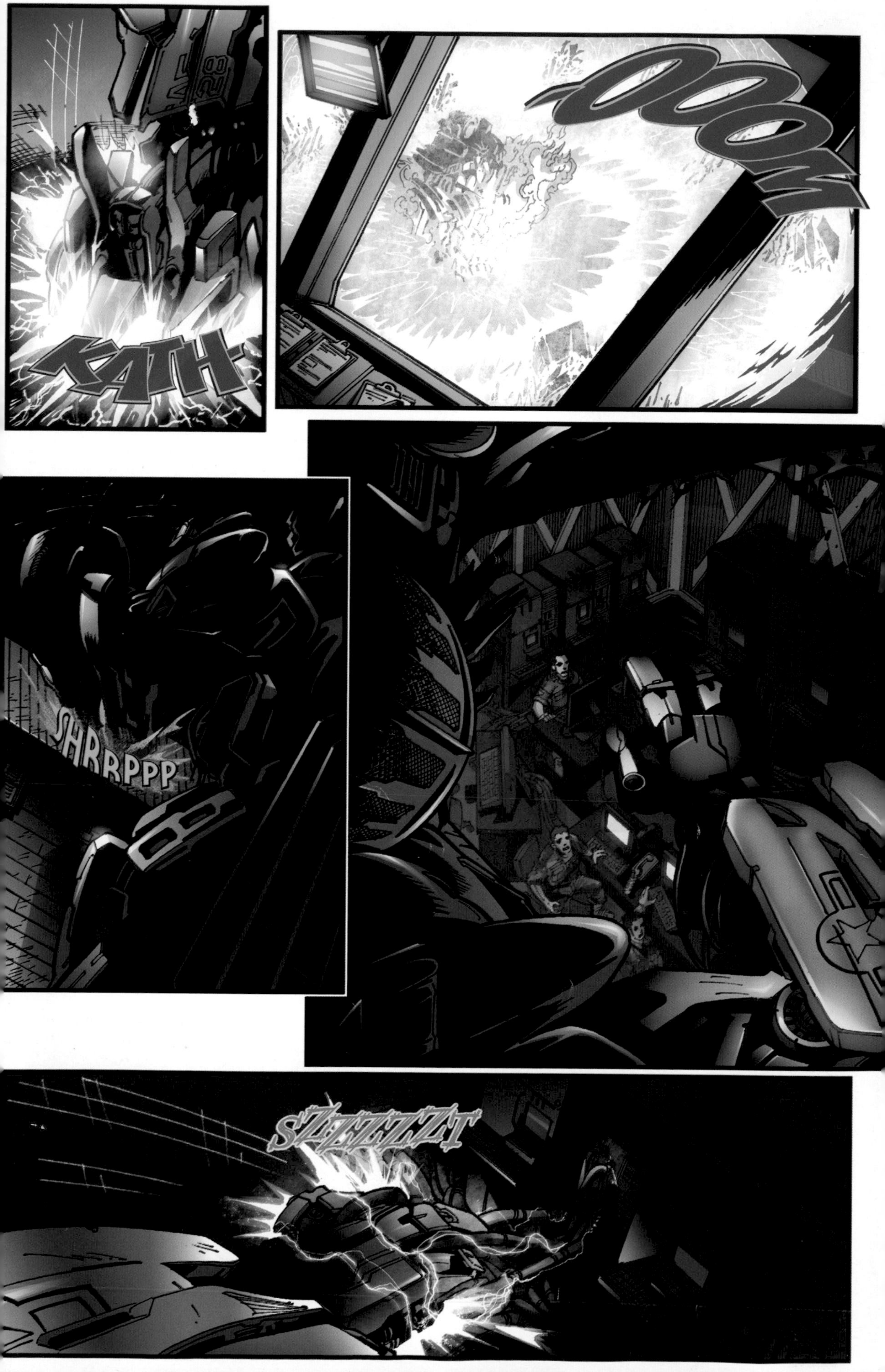
KATH
WOOOM
SHRRPPP
SZZZZZT

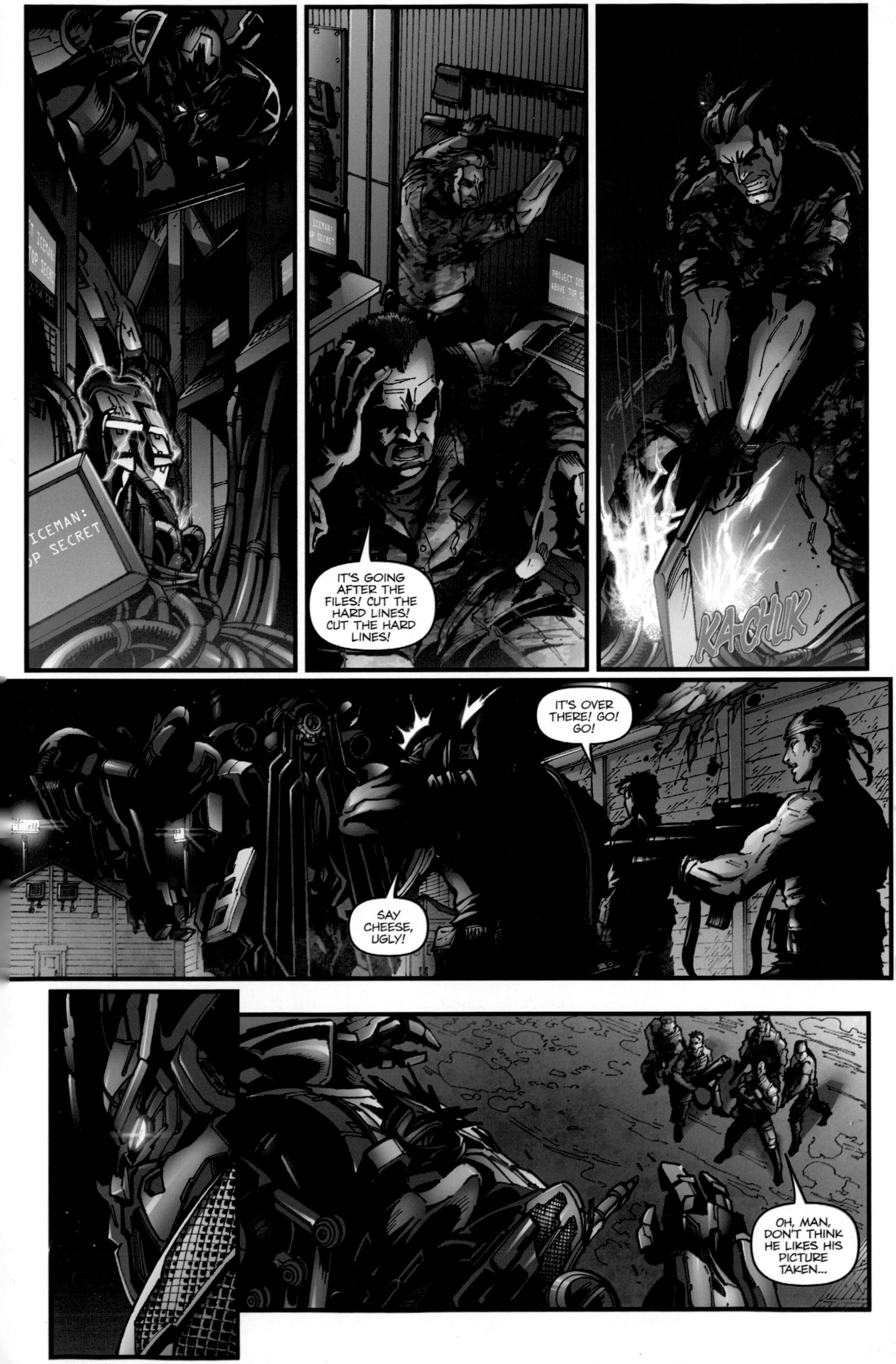
IT'S GOING AFTER THE FILES! CUT THE HARD LINES! CUT THE HARD LINES!
KA-CHUK
IT'S OVER THERE! GO! GO!
SAY CHEESE, UGLY!
OH, MAN, DON'T THINK HE LIKES HIS PICTURE TAKEN...

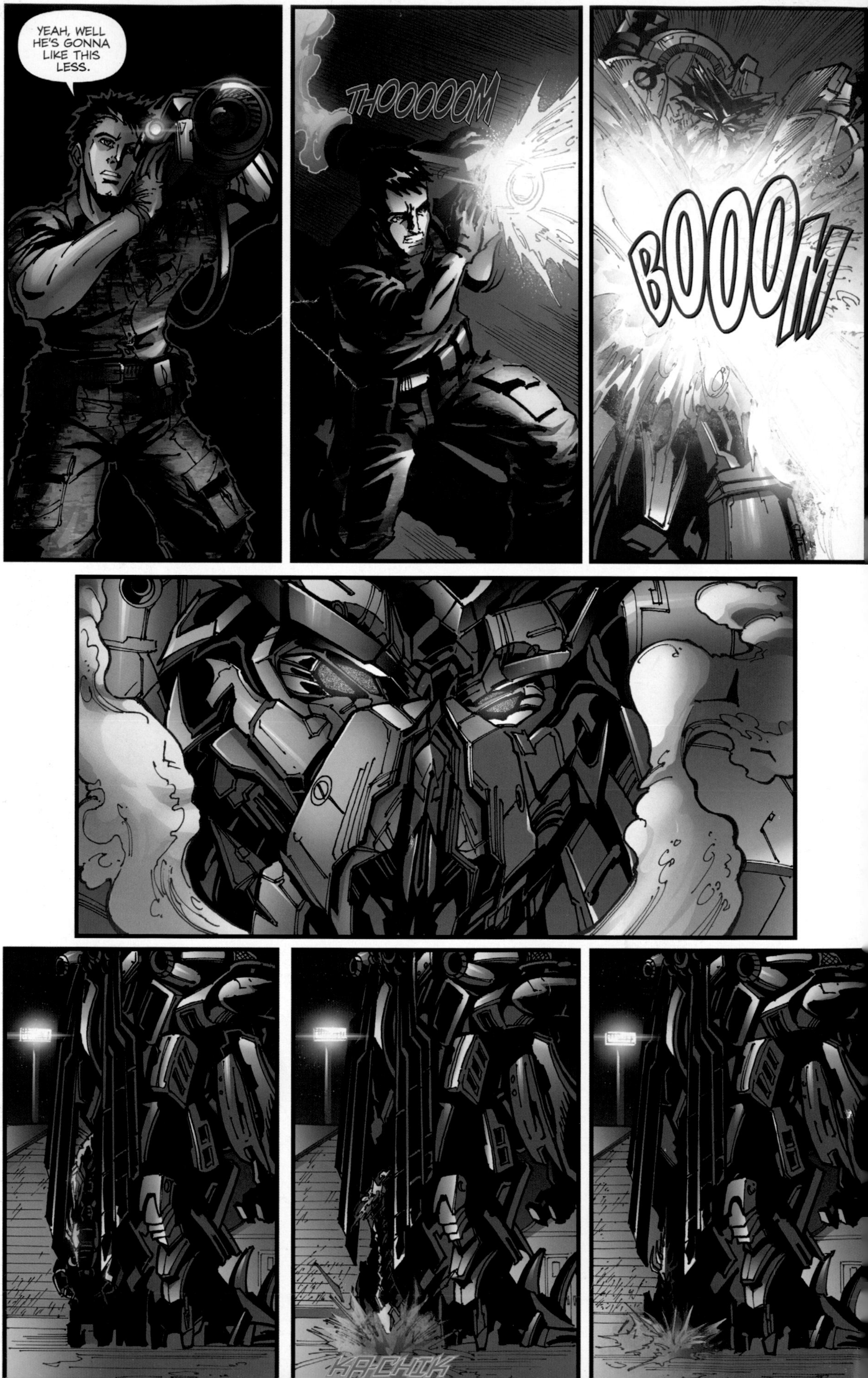
YEAH, WELL HE'S GONNA LIKE THIS LESS.
THOOOOOM
BOOOM
KA-CHIK

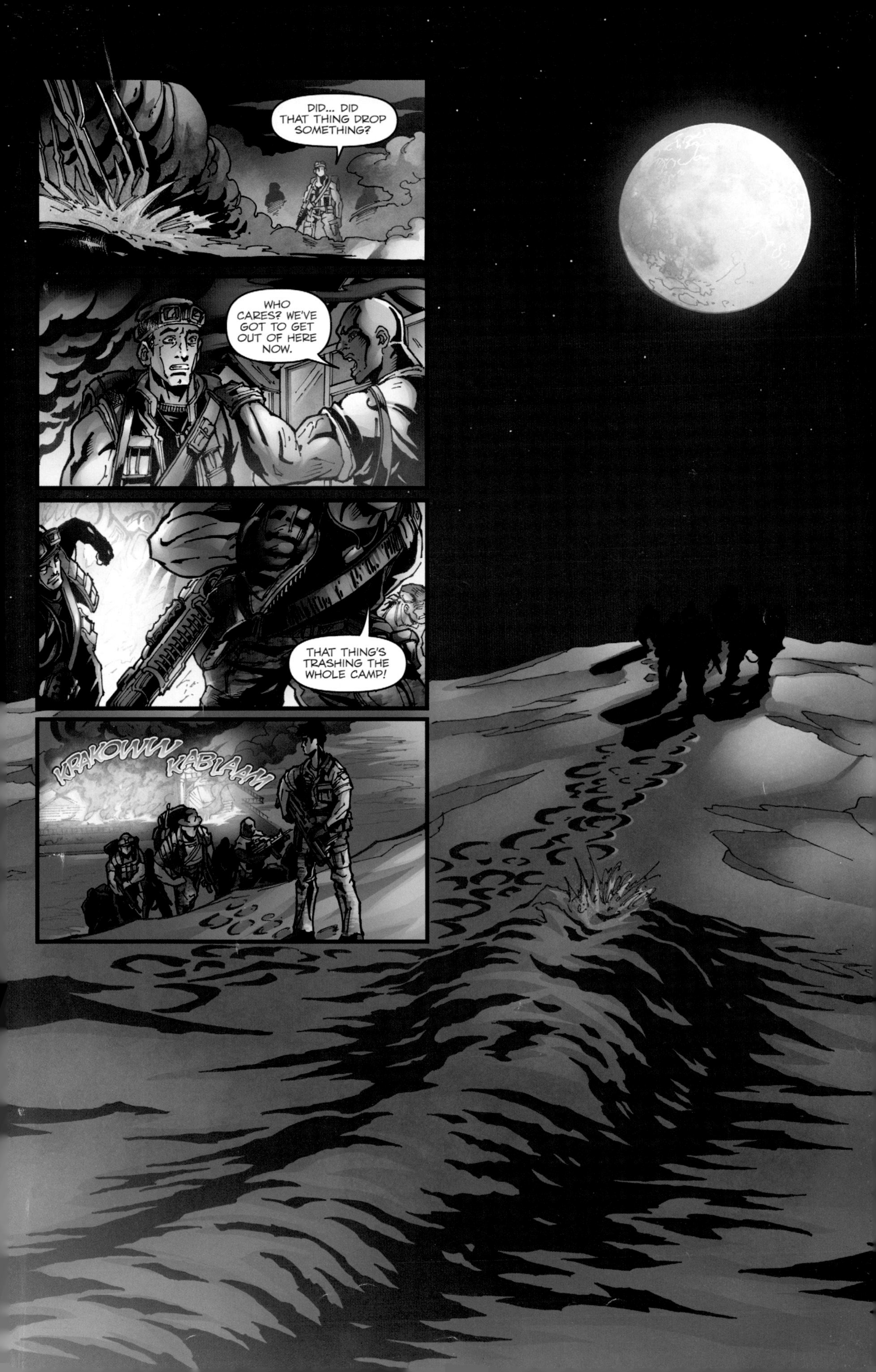
DID... DID THAT THING DROP SOMETHING?
WHO CARES? WE'VE GOT TO GET OUT OF HERE NOW.
THAT THING'S TRASHING THE WHOLE CAMP!
KRAKOWW
KABLAAM!

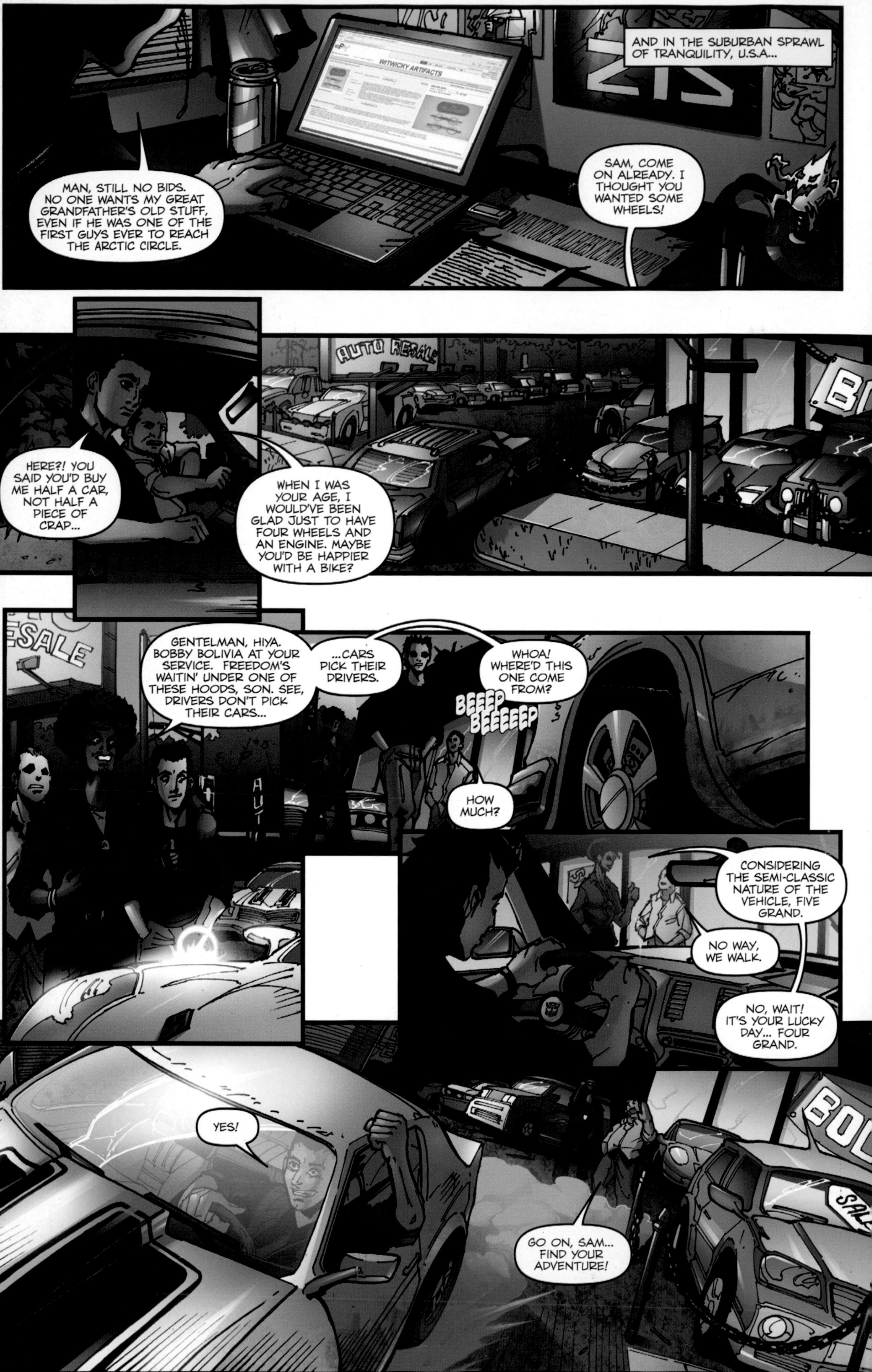
WITWICKY ARTIFACTS
AND IN THE SUBURBAN SPRAWL OF TRANQUILITY, U.S.A...
MAN, STILL NO BIDS. NO ONE WANTS MY GREAT GRANDFATHER'S OLD STUFF, EVEN IF HE WAS ONE OF THE FIRST GUYS EVER TO REACH THE ARCTIC CIRCLE.
SAM, COME ON ALREADY. I THOUGHT YOU WANTED SOME WHEELS!
AUTO RESALE
HERE?! YOU SAID YOU'D BUY ME HALF A CAR, NOT HALF A PIECE OF CRAP...
WHEN I WAS YOUR AGE, I WOULD'VE BEEN GLAD JUST TO HAVE FOUR WHEELS AND AN ENGINE. MAYBE YOU'D BE HAPPIER WITH A BIKE?
GENTELMAN, HIYA. BOBBY BOLIVIA AT YOUR SERVICE. FREEDOM'S WAITIN' UNDER ONE OF THESE HOODS, SON. SEE, DRIVERS DON'T PICK THEIR CARS...
...CARS PICK THEIR DRIVERS.
WHOA! WHERE'D THIS ONE COME FROM?
BEEEP BEEEEEP
HOW MUCH?
CONSIDERING THE SEMI-CLASSIC NATURE OF THE VEHICLE, FIVE GRAND.
NO WAY, WE WALK.
NO, WAIT! IT'S YOUR LUCKY DAY... FOUR GRAND.
YES!
GO ON, SAM... FIND YOUR ADVENTURE!

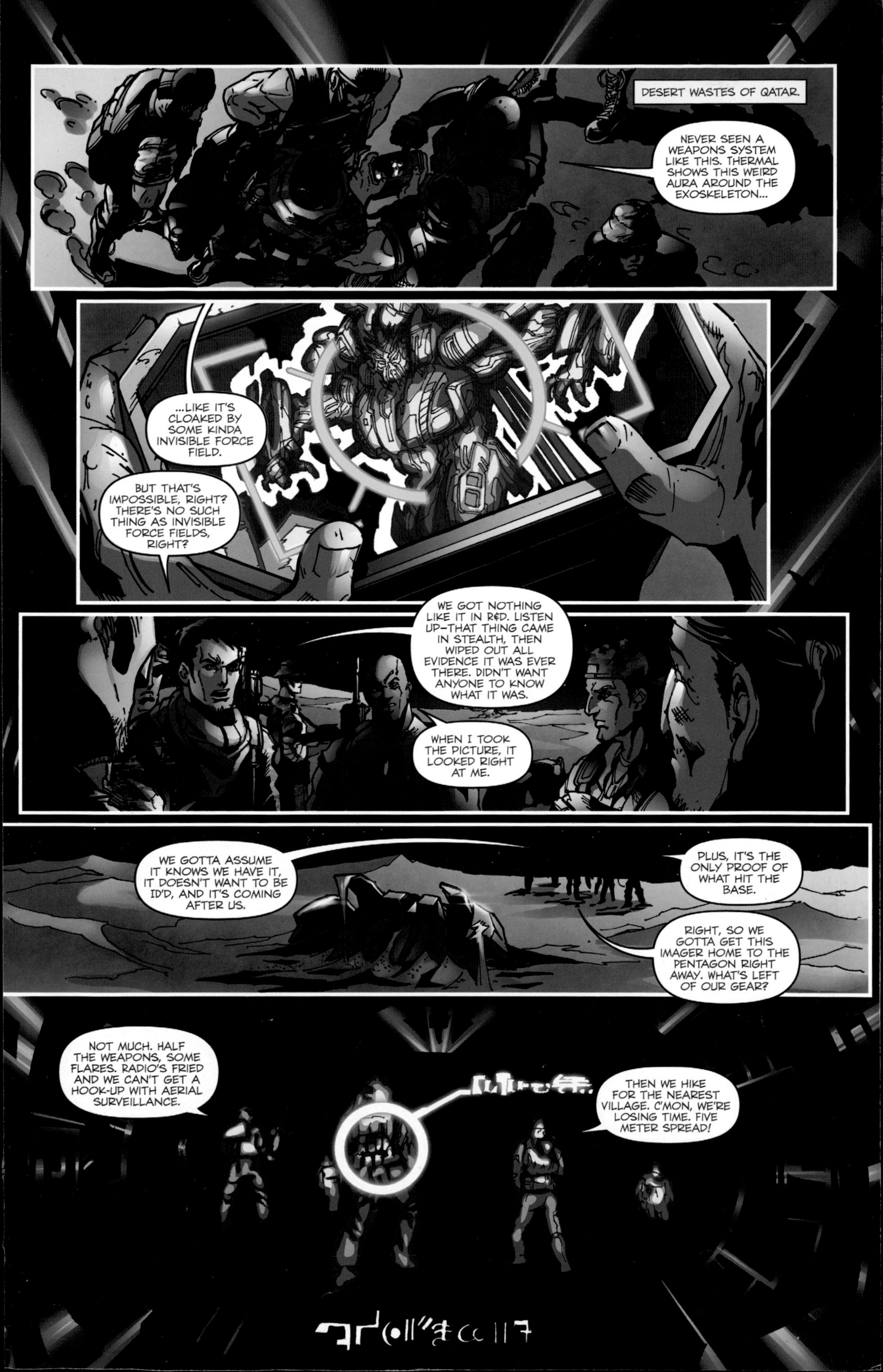
DESERT WASTES OF QATAR.
NEVER SEEN A WEAPONS SYSTEM LIKE THIS. THERMAL SHOWS THIS WEIRD AURA AROUND THE EXOSKELETON...
...LIKE IT'S CLOAKED BY SOME KINDA INVISIBLE FORCE FIELD.
BUT THAT'S IMPOSSIBLE, RIGHT? THERE'S NO SUCH THING AS INVISIBLE FORCE FIELDS, RIGHT?
WE GOT NOTHING LIKE IT IN R&D. LISTEN UP--THAT THING CAME IN STEALTH, THEN WIPED OUT ALL EVIDENCE IT WAS EVER THERE. DIDN'T WANT ANYONE TO KNOW WHAT IT WAS.
WHEN I TOOK THE PICTURE, IT LOOKED RIGHT AT ME.
WE GOTTA ASSUME IT KNOWS WE HAVE IT, IT DOESN'T WANT TO BE ID'D, AND IT'S COMING AFTER US.
PLUS, IT'S THE ONLY PROOF OF WHAT HIT THE BASE.
RIGHT, SO WE GOTTA GET THIS IMAGER HOME TO THE PENTAGON RIGHT AWAY. WHAT'S LEFT OF OUR GEAR?
NOT MUCH. HALF THE WEAPONS, SOME FLARES. RADIO'S FRIED AND WE CAN'T GET A HOOK-UP WITH AERIAL SURVEILLANCE.
THEN WE HIKE FOR THE NEAREST VILLAGE. C'MON, WE'RE LOSING TIME. FIVE METER SPREAD!

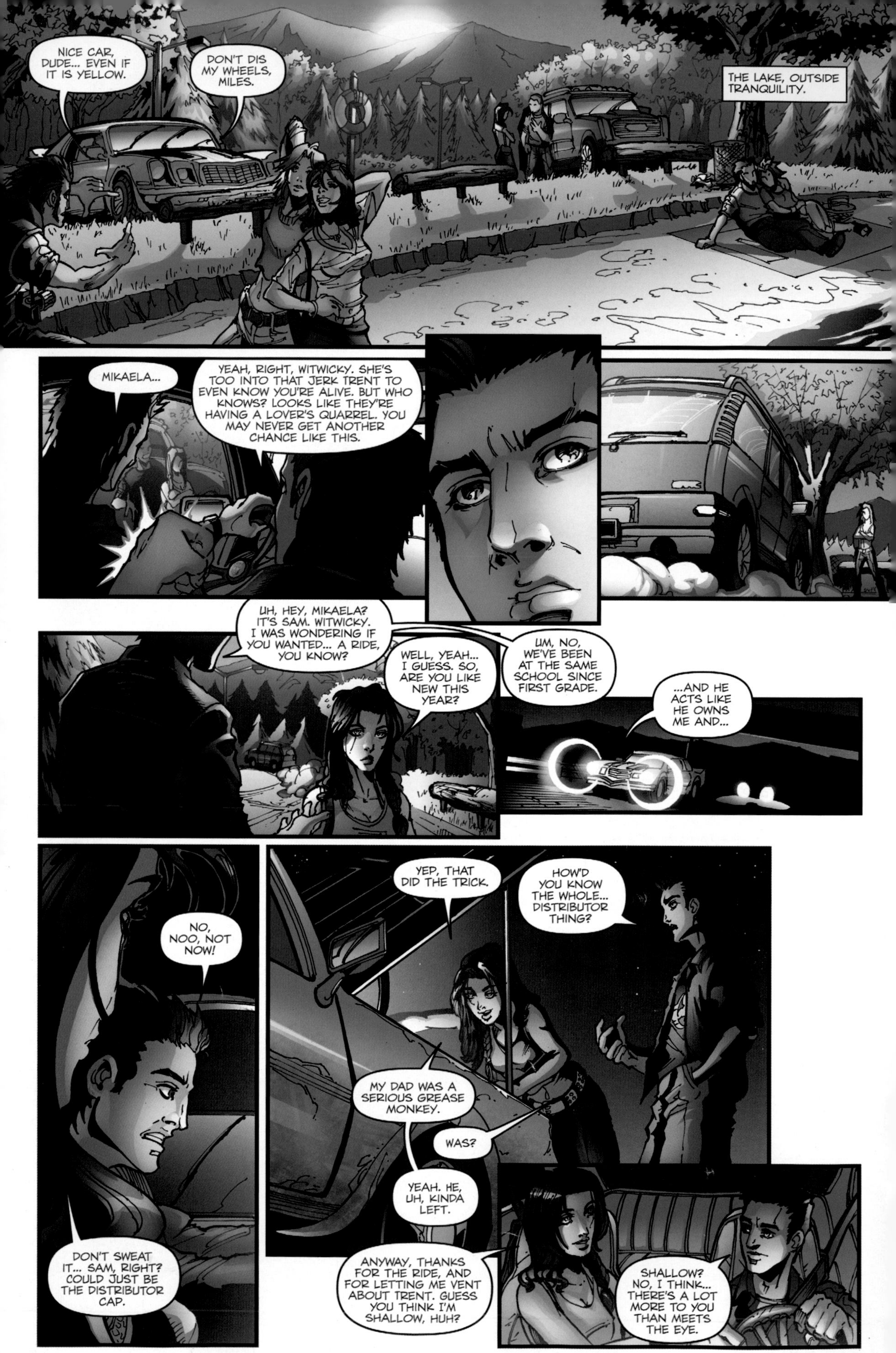
NICE CAR, DUDE... EVEN IF IT IS YELLOW.
DON'T DIS MY WHEELS, MILES.
THE LAKE, OUTSIDE TRANQUILITY.
MIKAELA...
YEAH, RIGHT, WITWICKY. SHE'S TOO INTO THAT JERK TRENT TO EVEN KNOW YOU'RE ALIVE. BUT WHO KNOWS? LOOKS LIKE THEY'RE HAVING A LOVER'S QUARREL. YOU MAY NEVER GET ANOTHER CHANCE LIKE THIS.
UH, HEY, MIKAELA? IT'S SAM. WITWICKY. I WAS WONDERING IF YOU WANTED... A RIDE, YOU KNOW?
WELL, YEAH... I GUESS. SO, ARE YOU LIKE NEW THIS YEAR?
UM, NO, WE'VE BEEN AT THE SAME SCHOOL SINCE FIRST GRADE.
...AND HE ACTS LIKE HE OWNS ME AND...
NO, NOO, NOT NOW!
DON'T SWEAT IT... SAM, RIGHT? COULD JUST BE THE DISTRIBUTOR CAP.
YEP, THAT DID THE TRICK.
HOW'D YOU KNOW THE WHOLE... DISTRIBUTOR THING?
MY DAD WAS A SERIOUS GREASE MONKEY.
WAS?
YEAH. HE, UH, KINDA LEFT.
ANYWAY, THANKS FOR THE RIDE, AND FOR LETTING ME VENT ABOUT TRENT. GUESS YOU THINK I'M SHALLOW, HUH?
SHALLOW? NO, I THINK... THERE'S A LOT MORE TO YOU THAN MEETS THE EYE.

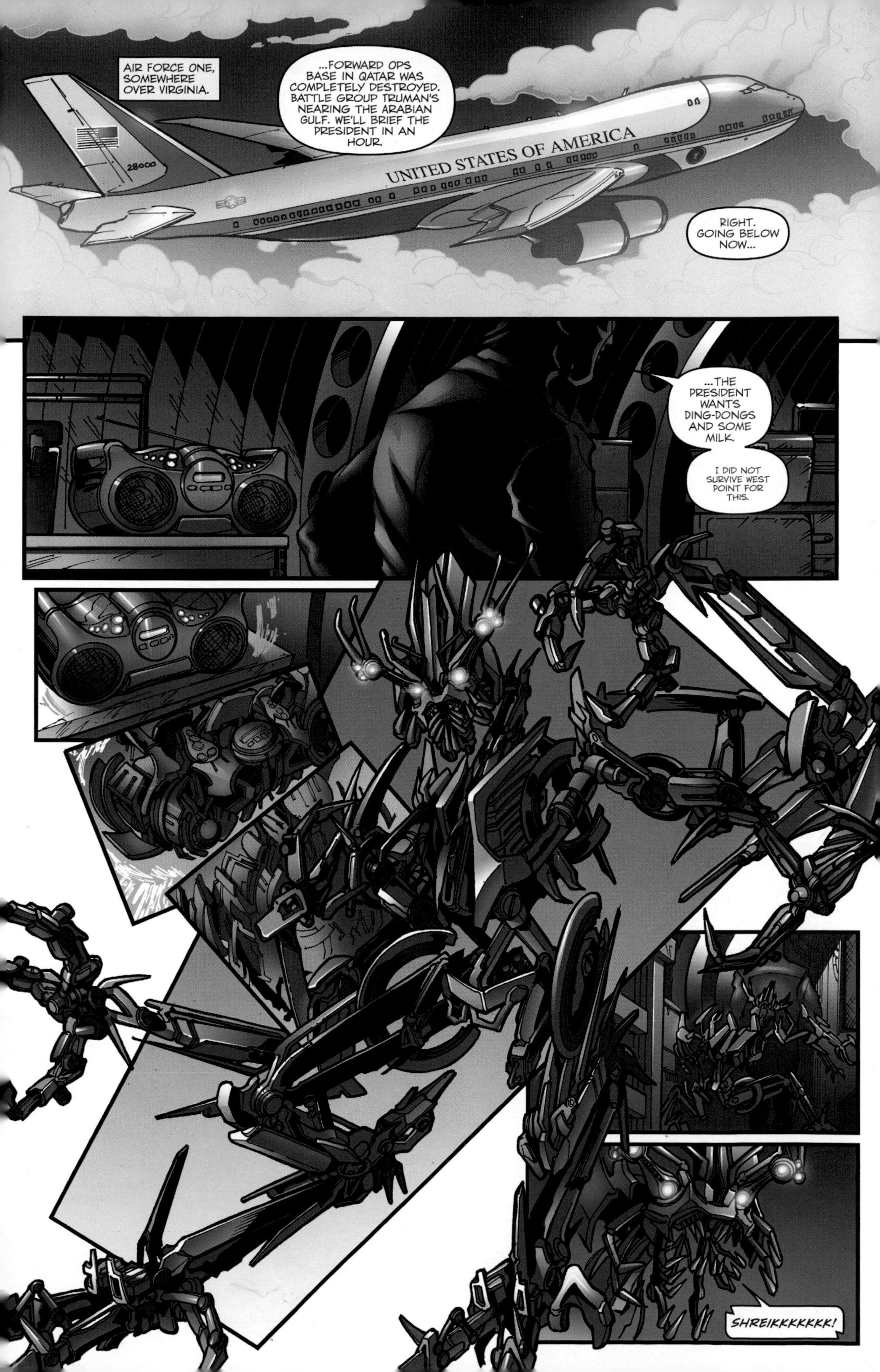
AIR FORCE ONE, SOMEWHERE OVER VIRGINIA.
...FORWARD OPS BASE IN QATAR WAS COMPLETELY DESTROYED. BATTLE GROUP TRUMAN'S NEARING THE ARABIAN GULF. WE'LL BRIEF THE PRESIDENT IN AN HOUR.
UNITED STATES OF AMERICA
RIGHT. GOING BELOW NOW...
...THE PRESIDENT WANTS DING-DONGS AND SOME MILK.
I DID NOT SURVIVE WEST POINT FOR THIS.
SHREIKKKKKKK!

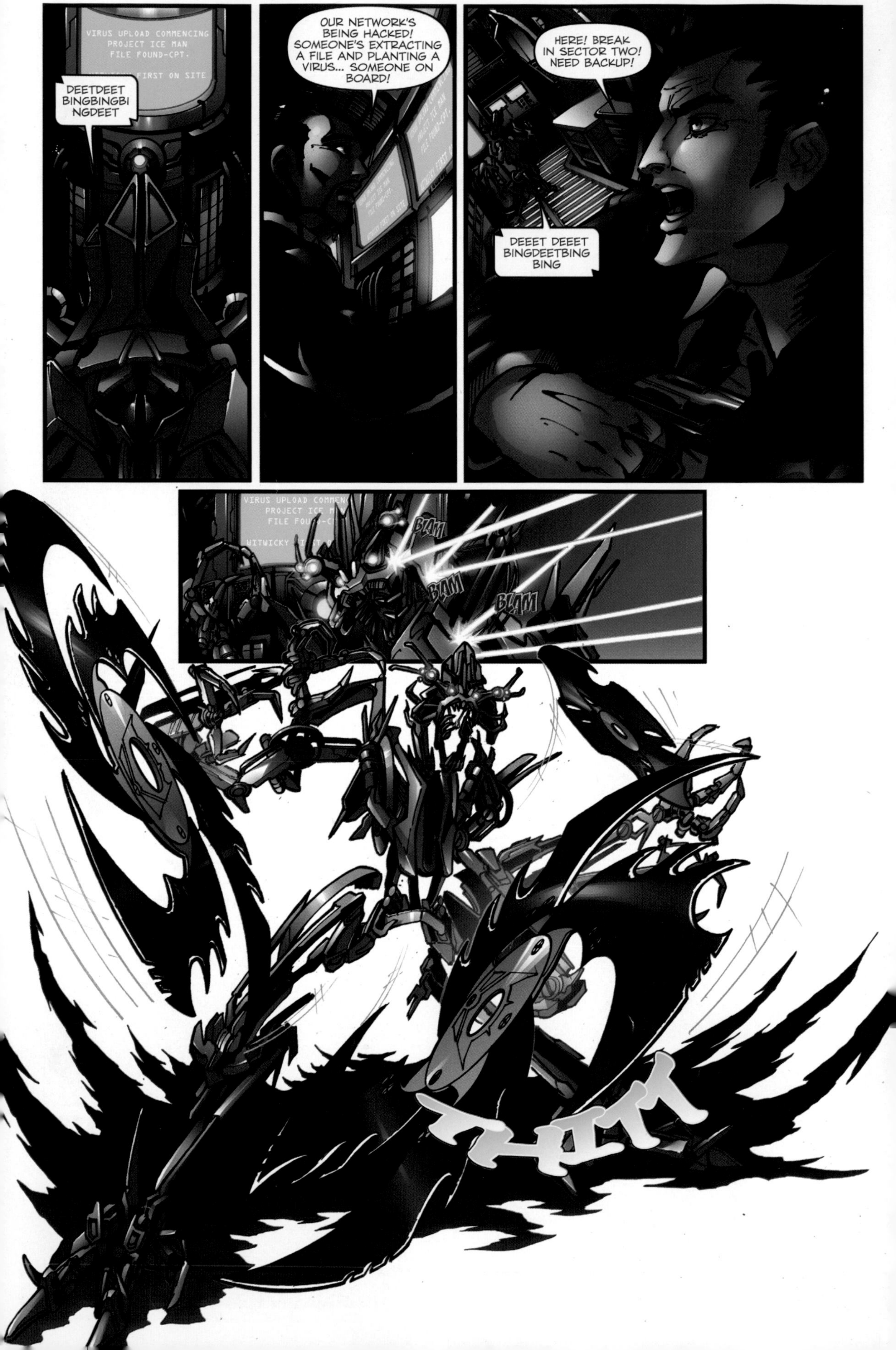

VIRUS UPLOAD COMMENCING
PROJECT ICE MAN
FILE FOUND-CPT.
DEETDEET BINGBINGBI NGDEET
OUR NETWORK'S BEING HACKED! SOMEONE'S EXTRACTING A FILE AND PLANTING A VIRUS... SOMEONE ON BOARD!
HERE! BREAK IN SECTOR TWO! NEED BACKUP!
DEEET DEEET BINGDEETBING BING
BLAM
BLAM
BLAM

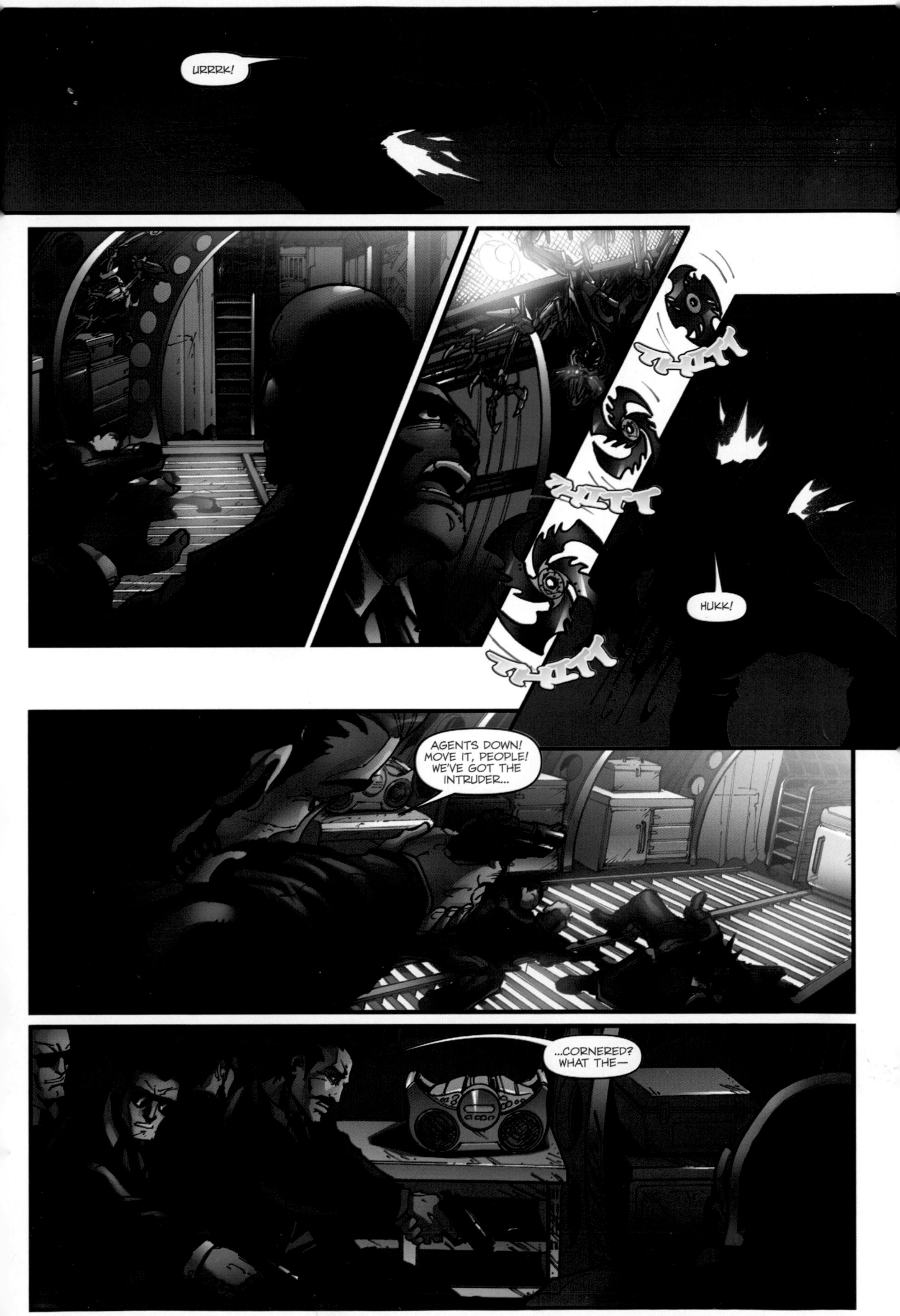
URRRK!
THTT
THTT
THTT
HUKK!
AGENTS DOWN! MOVE IT, PEOPLE! WE'VE GOT THE INTRUDER...
...CORNERED? WHAT THE—

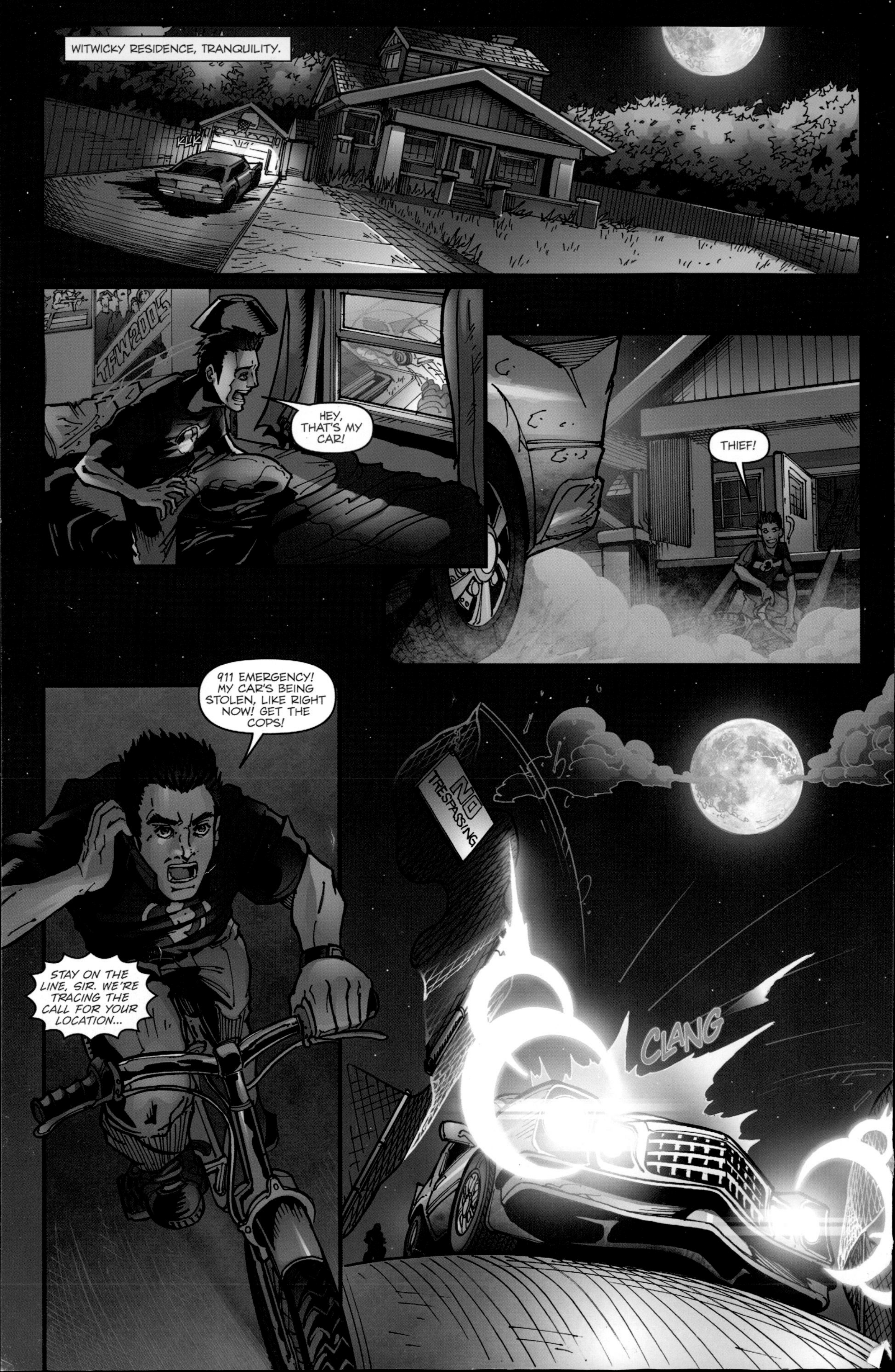
WITWICKY RESIDENCE, TRANQUILITY.
KUK
TFW2005
HEY, THAT'S MY CAR!
THIEF!
911 EMERGENCY! MY CAR'S BEING STOLEN, LIKE RIGHT NOW! GET THE COPS!
STAY ON THE LINE, SIR. WE'RE TRACING THE CALL FOR YOUR LOCATION...
NO TRESPASSING
CLANG

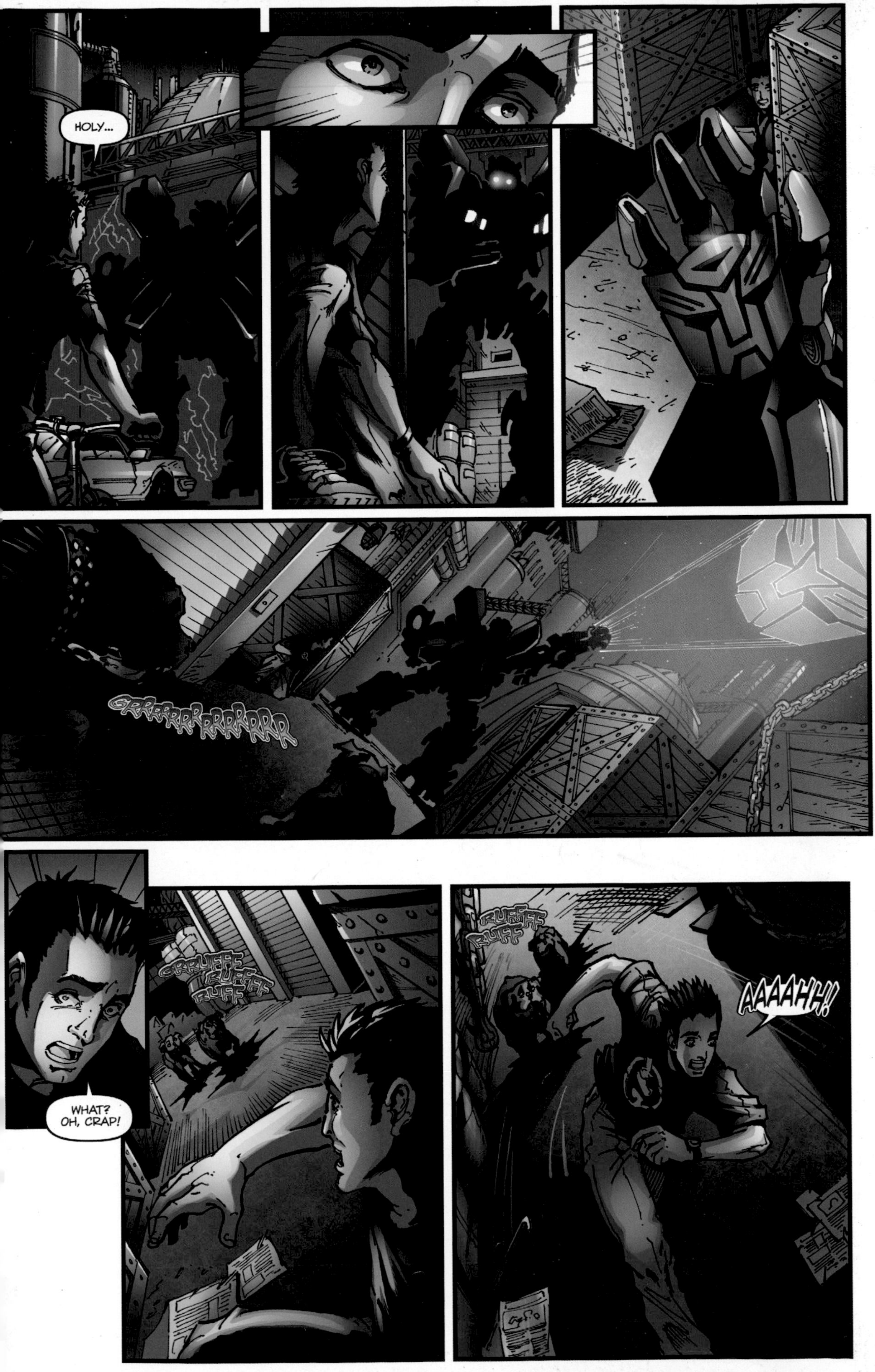
HOLY...
GRRRRRRRRRRRRRR
WHAT? OH, CRAP!
GRRUFFF RUFFF RUFF
RUFFF RUFF
AAAAHH!

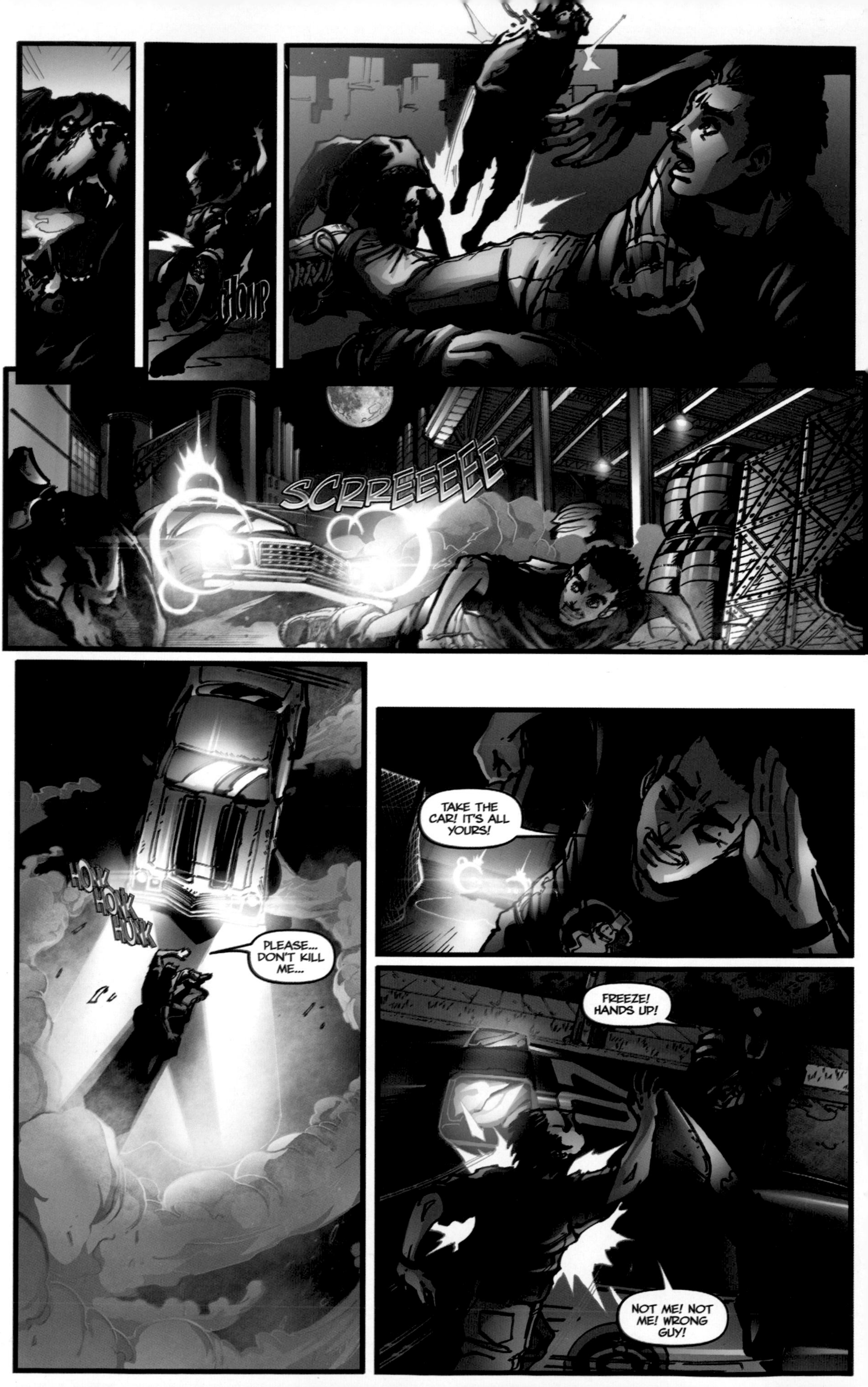
THOMP
SCRREEEEEE
HONK HONK HONK
PLEASE... DON'T KILL ME...
TAKE THE CAR! IT'S ALL YOURS!
FREEZE! HANDS UP!
NOT ME! NOT ME! WRONG GUY!

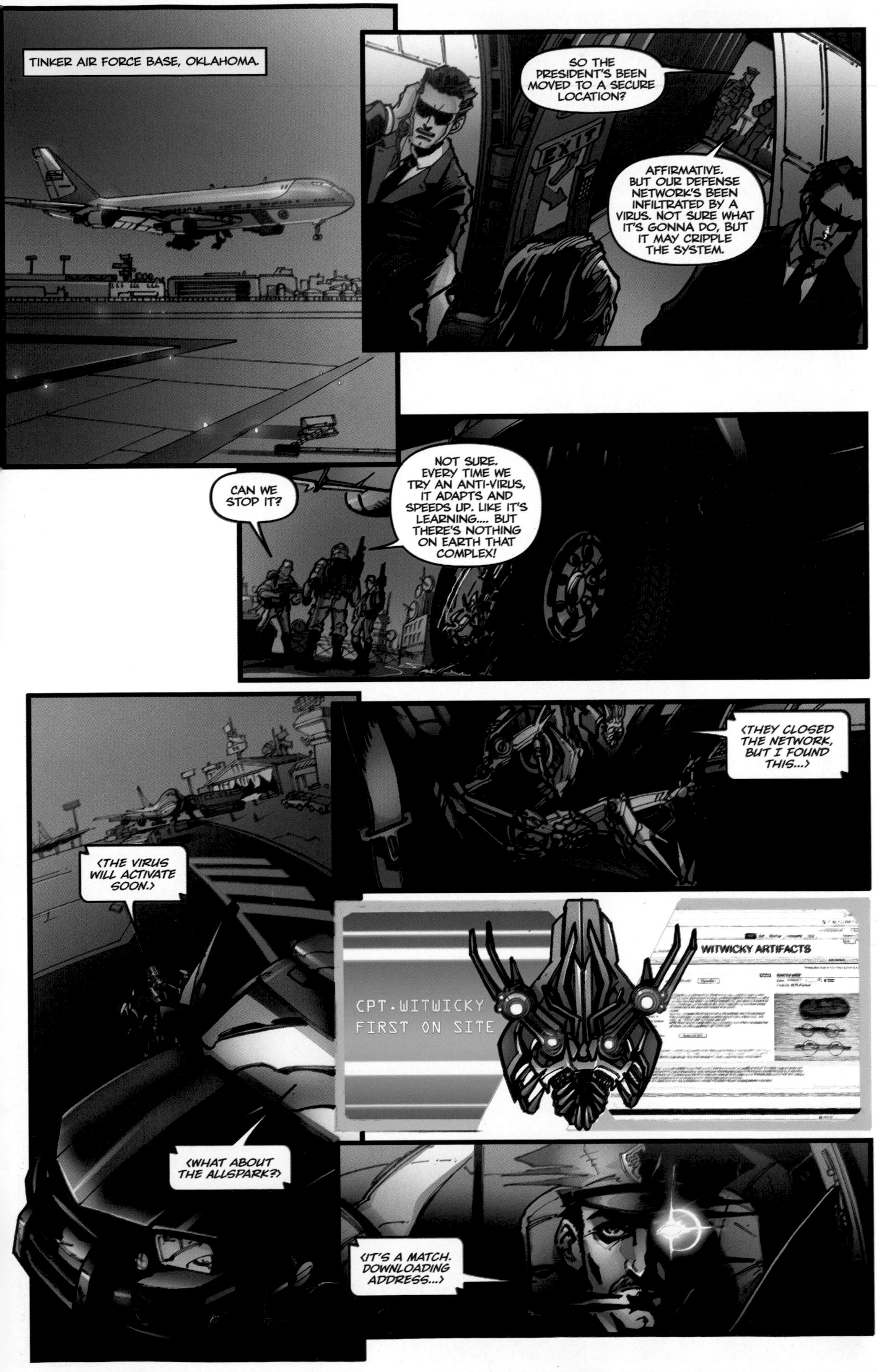
TINKER AIR FORCE BASE, OKLAHOMA.
SO THE PRESIDENT'S BEEN MOVED TO A SECURE LOCATION?
AFFIRMATIVE. BUT OUR DEFENSE NETWORK'S BEEN INFILTRATED BY A VIRUS. NOT SURE WHAT IT'S GONNA DO, BUT IT MAY CRIPPLE THE SYSTEM.
EXIT
CAN WE STOP IT?
NOT SURE. EVERY TIME WE TRY AN ANTI-VIRUS, IT ADAPTS AND SPEEDS UP. LIKE IT'S LEARNING.... BUT THERE'S NOTHING ON EARTH THAT COMPLEX!
‹THE VIRUS WILL ACTIVATE SOON.›
‹THEY CLOSED THE NETWORK, BUT I FOUND THIS...›
CPT. WITWICKY FIRST ON SITE
WITWICKY ARTIFACTS
‹WHAT ABOUT THE ALLSPARK?›
‹IT'S A MATCH. DOWNLOADING ADDRESS...›

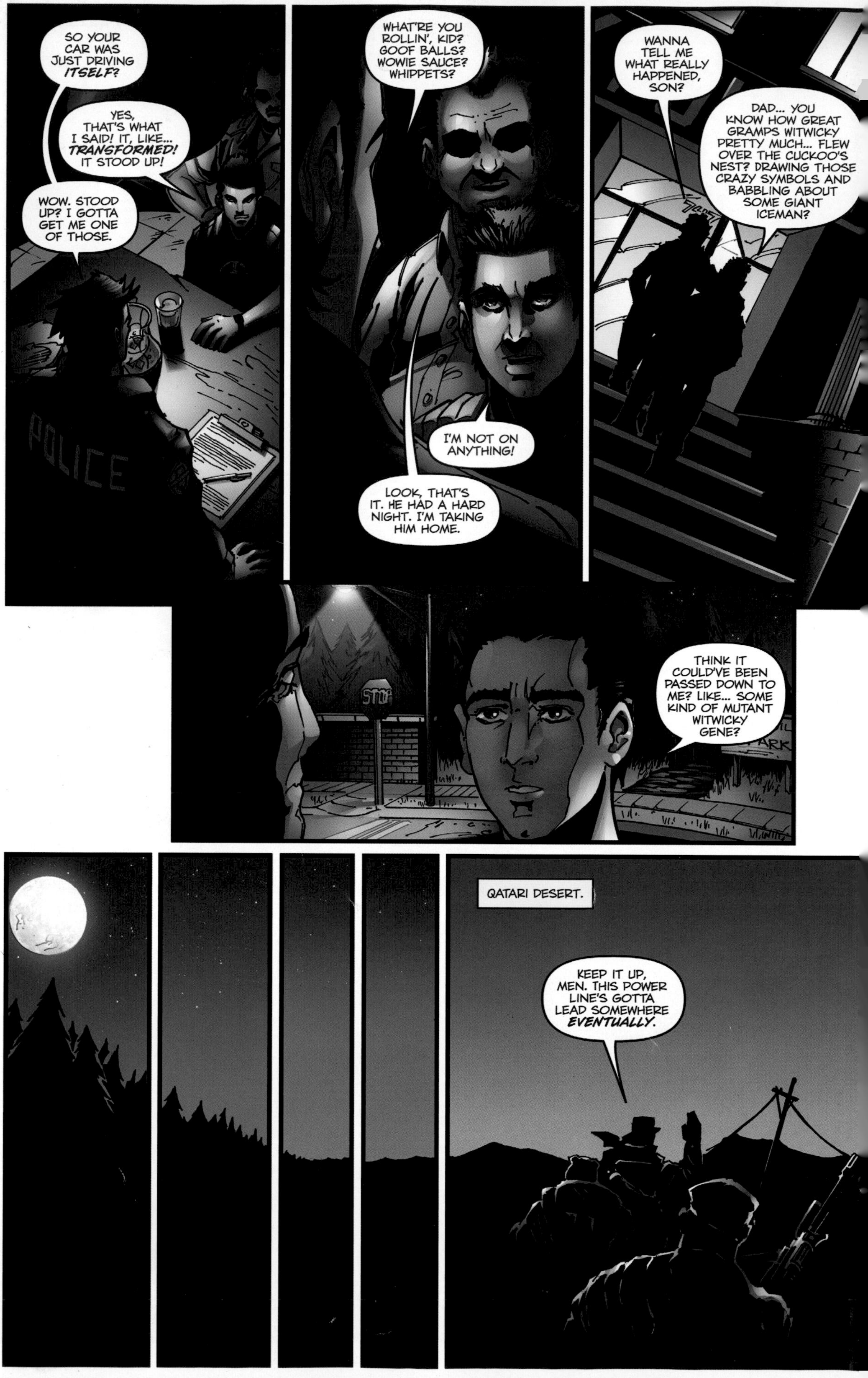
SO YOUR CAR WAS JUST DRIVING *ITSELF*?
YES, THAT'S WHAT I SAID! IT, LIKE... *TRANSFORMED!* IT STOOD UP!
WOW. STOOD UP? I GOTTA GET ME ONE OF THOSE.
POLICE
WHAT'RE YOU ROLLIN', KID? GOOF BALLS? WOWIE SAUCE? WHIPPETS?
I'M NOT ON ANYTHING!
LOOK, THAT'S IT. HE HAD A HARD NIGHT. I'M TAKING HIM HOME.
WANNA TELL ME WHAT REALLY HAPPENED, SON?
DAD... YOU KNOW HOW GREAT GRAMPS WITWICKY PRETTY MUCH... FLEW OVER THE CUCKOO'S NEST? DRAWING THOSE CRAZY SYMBOLS AND BABBLING ABOUT SOME GIANT ICEMAN?
THINK IT COULD'VE BEEN PASSED DOWN TO ME? LIKE... SOME KIND OF MUTANT WITWICKY GENE?
QATARI DESERT.
KEEP IT UP, MEN. THIS POWER LINE'S GOTTA LEAD SOMEWHERE *EVENTUALLY*.

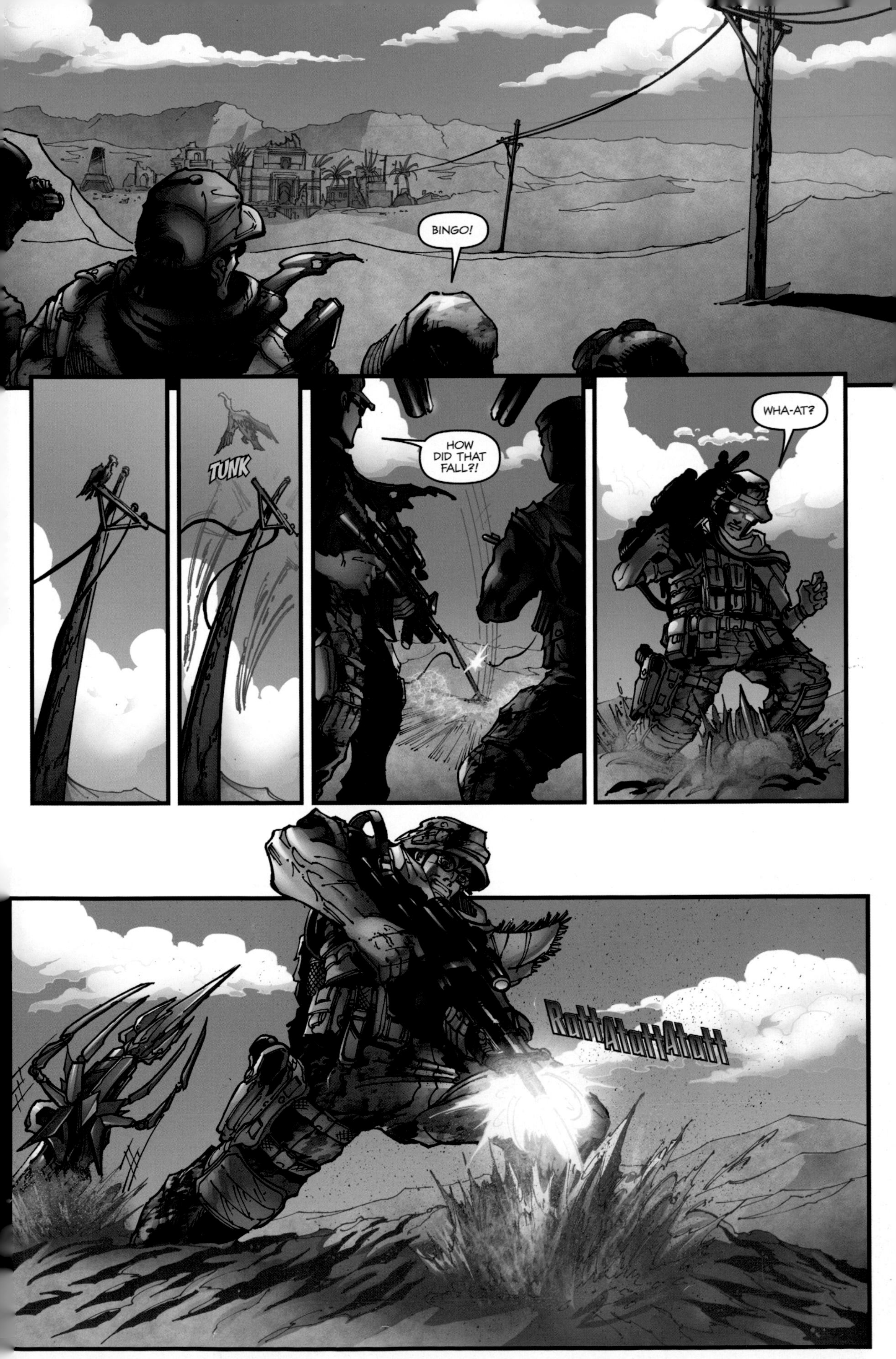
BINGO!
TUNK
HOW DID THAT FALL?!
WHA-AT?
RattAtattAtatt

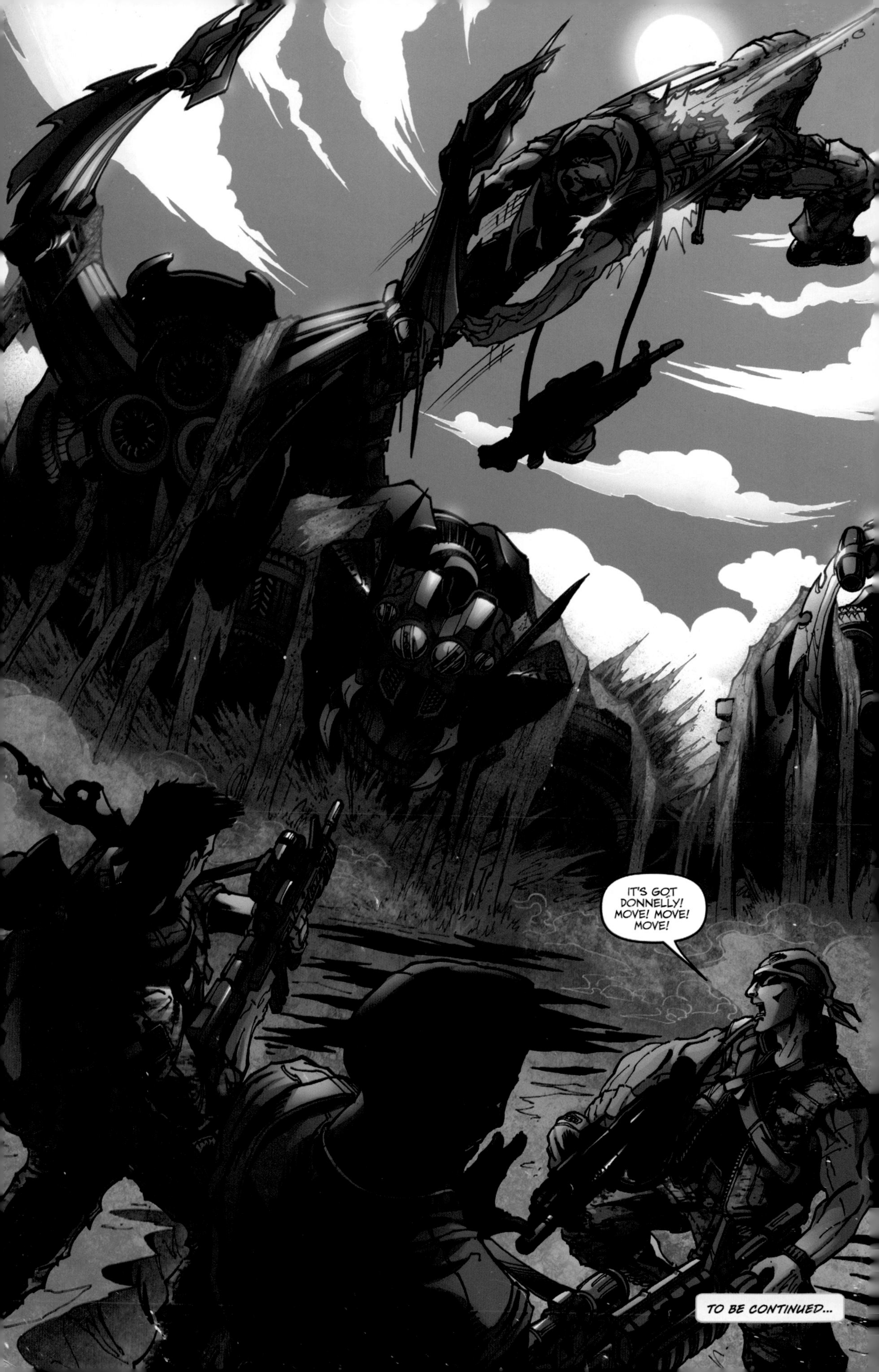
IT'S GOT DONNELLY! MOVE! MOVE! MOVE!
TO BE CONTINUED...